A String of Hearts

WITHDRAWN

By Laura Malone Elliott

Illustrated by Lynn Munsinger

KATHERINE TEGEN BOOKS
An Imprint of HarperCollins Publishers

Katherine Tegen Books is an imprint of HarperCollins Publishers.

A String of Hearts
Text copyright © 2010 by Laura Malone Elliott
Illustrations copyright © 2010 by Lynn Munsinger
All rights reserved. Manufactured in China.

Library of Congress Cataloging-in-Publication Data is available.
ISBN 978-0-06-000085-1 (trade bdg.) — ISBN 978-0-06-000086-8 (lib. bdg.)

Typography by Rachel Zegar
10 11 12 13 14 LEO 10 9 8 7 6 5 4 3 2 1
❖
First Edition

To my valentines, Peter, Megan, and John

—L.M.E.

For Abigail

—L.M.

Tomorrow was the class Valentine's Day party.
"Make a valentine for everyone," said Sam's
teacher, Mrs. Wright. "Write something special
about each classmate."

Sam groaned. What nice thing could he write about Nicole? Nicole had said his really cool light-up tennis shoes were dumb looking.

Sam wiggled his toes. He loved those shoes.

Sam looked over at Tiffany. Saying something nice about
her would be easy. Tiffany always looked pretty in purple—
purple bows, purple boots, purple skirts.

When the class did a project about favorite colors, everyone said theirs was purple. Even the boys.

Everyone except Sam's next-door neighbor,
Mary Ann. She'd picked chartreuse.

Once Sam noticed Tiffany drop her favorite pencil. When Sam returned it, she called him "sweet."

"Maybe my valentine will make her notice me again," Sam said hopefully.

"Hey, Tiff," Winston called, "look at me!" Winston flipped himself into a handstand and made a silly face. Tiffany giggled. Then all the girls giggled, too.

Jeffrey offered to carry her books. Tiffany said *he* was "sweet." The other girls *awwww*ed.

Tiffany left school with Winston on one side and Jeffrey on the other. The other girls followed behind. Sam needed to make a *really* great Valentine.

All the way home he worried.

"Hey, Sam, wait up!" Mary Ann skipped up from behind him.

"What's bothering you?" she asked.
"I need to make a really good valentine."
"Really?" Mary Ann smiled. "Who for?"
He whispered, "Tiffany."

Mary Ann's face fell. But then she
said, "Well, I read a book about making
valentines. I'll show you how."
Sam felt better already.

On her kitchen table, Mary Ann spread out construction paper, lace doilies, glue, scissors, ribbons, crayons, and a shoe box full of stickers.

She made a red heart by folding a piece of paper in half and cutting a teardrop on the fold. When she unfolded the teardrop, it made a heart.

"Wow!" said Sam. He watched her glue the heart on a white card and draw an arrow through it in silver crayon. She wrote in big letters: "Be my valentine."

Sam stuck soccer-ball stickers all over a piece of paper. He wrote: "You are a kick."

"That's a great valentine for Nicole," said Mary Ann. Nicole was the class star soccer player. "But Tiffany doesn't play soccer."

Sam picked up a new piece of paper and started drawing.

Mary Ann threaded a pink ribbon through the edges of a lace doily. She pasted a pink heart in its center and wrote M-O-M. She used each letter to begin a line:

Makes me feel special.

Outstanding in every way.

Much love I give you on Valentine's Day!

Sam held up his drawing. "Be my alien," said the monster.

Mary Ann laughed. "That's perfect for Winston. He wants to be an astronaut." Mary Ann kept to herself that she kind of, sort of wished Tiffany would go to outer space instead.

Sam started over.

With her pencil, Mary Ann pinpricked
the outline of a heart in shiny foil paper.

She wrote to her big brother:

You taught me to climb trees
and how to shell a peanut.
I will love you always,
'cause you're cool like King Tut.

Sam used a poem the boys recited:

> Roses are red,
> violets are blue.
> Your feet are big,
> and they smell bad, too.

"Sam! Smelly feet aren't going to work with Tiffany. A valentine should say *why* you like a person, what's special about her. So what does Tiffany like, besides purple?"

Sam thought and thought. He really didn't know much about Tiffany.

"Let's stick with purple then." Mary Ann looked in the shoe box. She found lots of purple stickers.

Sam took a large piece of gold paper, pasted a doily on it, a heart on that, and surrounded it with the stickers.

It was beautiful.

"She'll love it, Sam," said Mary Ann quietly. "It's the nicest valentine I've ever seen."

At the Valentine's Day party everyone crowded around Tiffany.
Winston gave her a valentine with a rose taped on it.

Jeffrey gave her a big chocolate heart.
All the girls gave her valentines covered with purple lollipops.

Finally Sam handed Tiffany his valentine.
"Thank you, Sam," said Tiffany.

Her arms were so full, Tiffany dropped Sam's
valentine. She never noticed.

Sadly, Sam picked up his valentine and stuffed it in his coat. But inside his pocket he found something else. It was a valentine, and it opened up in a string of hearts. Each heart had a line:

> I like you because . . .
> You made me cookies when I had chicken pox.
> You can make pretend spaceships from a box.
> You like to fly kites up high.
> And you never, ever lie.

It was signed: Mary Ann.

Sam caught his breath. He hadn't been able to think
of a thing to put on Tiffany's card. But suddenly he could
think of a hundred things to write Mary Ann.

He liked the way she played basketball and Monopoly and
read so many books. She had carried his school lunch tray when
he broke his arm and had talked him into learning to swim.

Sam ran home and found a piece of red construction paper. He folded it in half and drew hearts all over it.

He titled it: "The Book on Mary Ann." Inside he wrote: "I love how you always make me feel better."

He slipped it into her mailbox.

The next morning, Sam and Mary Ann walked to school together.

"Thanks for the valentine, Sam."

"You're welcome," he answered.

She smiled.

He turned red.

Sam changed the subject. "What is chartru-charwhatamacallit, anyway?"

"*Chartreuse*? I read about it in a book. It's a light green with a little yellow in it." She skipped ahead of him and called back, "Like the color of your eyes."

"Hey, Mary Ann," Sam called. "Wait up!"

A Note About Valentine's Day

St. Valentine was a priest who married couples in secret during the rule of a Roman emperor called Claudius the Cruel. Claudius thought his soldiers would be better fighters if they didn't have sweethearts, so he outlawed marriage. Valentine was arrested. Legend says he fell in love with his jailer's blind daughter. He wrote her a note telling her how he felt. Suddenly she could see to read: "from your Valentine."

In the Middle Ages, people celebrated Valentine's Day using customs from the Roman festival Lupercalia, honoring love. Boys drew girls' names from bowls and wore them on their sleeves. Children went to houses, singing, "Good morning, Valentine," and adults gave them sweet buns. Migrating birds returned in mid-February to choose a mate. That's how Valentine's Day came to be February 14 and why doves appear on valentines. People wrote poems to their beloved, decorating them with flowers, hearts, ribbons, and Cupids—the mischievous Roman god who shot arrows of love.

During the 1800s in England, people made fancy cards with lace and pearl ornaments. Cards were red, white, and pink—red for the heart, white for loyalty, and pink for the almond tree that bloomed when St. Valentine died. Valentines caught on in the United States during the Civil War. Cards opened like tent flaps to show a soldier inside, reminding sweethearts to stay true. In 1850, Esther Howland started selling the first premade valentines. Today, February 14 is the post office's busiest day: 200 million cards are posted, like those made by Esther. But many people still believe handmade cards are nicest.